Chapter 1: All fools fall in love

Davon was a 20 years old living at home

with his mother. Davon loved to write

music. One day he was at the studio and

he recorded a song called "Invisible".

Davon had problems finding a girlfriend

all his life. His problem was he couldn't

find a good job. He was getting money by

selling his music on CDs. While out selling

his music he met a woman. The woman

was beautiful to him. She had nice full

lips, dimples, and she wore braces. Her

name was Asset.

Asset notices Davon and approached

him as she seen him being energetic, and making sells with his music. "Hey can I buy one" says Asset with a soft voice. Davon looks at her in surprise "yea of course you can they're ten dollars". As she grabs the CD and pays him she says "do you have social media or anything". Davon quickly responds.

"Yes King Davon. That's my social media name add me". "I will King Davon"; says Asset. Later that day Davon goes to his friend Joe Kush to grab him some weed. Davon yells "kush"! "My dawg what's good". Says Joe Kush. As Davon pulls out his wallet he says "let me get a quarter of that Alpoko off you fam". "Say less", said joe. Joe bags up a quarter of weed. "What's new with you fam". Says

Joe. Davon responds with a sigh

"Same ol bro, just trying to stay a float".

As Joe hands him the weed he says

"make sure you do that fam real shit".

Davon takes the weed and heads home.

As he checks his phone, he see a

request from Asset. He immediately

inboxed her. He asked her to meet him at

a restaurant. He didn't have much money

after grabbing weed. He had about eighty

dollars. He took her out to a inexpensive

restaurant, and made her laugh and they

talked for 3 hours at the restaurant. They

eventually started to date. Davon didnt tell

her he didn't have a job. One day she

came up to him. "Bae can I get like forty

dollars" says Asset. Davon knowing he

didn't have much gave it to her.

It was his last forty dollars.

The next day he was going out to

sell CDs and he made ninety dollars.

When he Got home Asset was calling.

"Bae can I get forty dollars I need to get

some gas and grab some food for work.

He knowing that was almost half his

money said "I got you baby come grab it"

When she got there she went up stairs

and she pushed him on his bed and took

his clothes off. She took all her clothes

and began to have sex with him very

intensely. He turned her over and

smacked her butt. He grabbed her chest

and bit her on the neck as he stroked her

until she climaxed.

The next day he end up having

to buy a few things and spent all his

money. Later Asset called. "Bae I really

need forty dollars so I can get my phone fixed i dropped it at work". "Baby I don't got it". Davon says. "When do you get paid again" asset says confused. "I don't have a job other than selling my music right now" says Davon. "Bae let me call you back this my grandma" says asset. After they get off the phone time goes by and Asset doesn't call.

Davon decides to call and it goes straight to voicemail. The next day he tries to call again, and this time the phone number is changed. He didn't know where she stayed so he had no way of contacting her. He goes back out to sell his CDs. While he out he sees a guy pull up to the gas station he was standing at in a brand new Beamer. He gets out the car and walks towards the store. "What's

good big bro. I don't mean to bother you I just wanted to see if you wanted grab a copy of my Album its Ten dollars". Says Davon. "What you talking about young cuz?". Says Jon. "Man I only rap about the stuff I been through and how I cope" Davon adds. As Jon looks calm he says "Ok give me fifty of em". Davon in shock "that's exactly how many I got left are you serious". "Yes i am i love to support hustlers". Says Jon. After that Davon made five hundred bucks. Later that night Davon gets a call. He answers "hello". "Bae I'm sorry my phone got cut off. I was hoping I could get forty dollars". Says Asset.
Davon in excitement responds "Baby I was worried are you ok and yes I got you come get it". Asset arrives

And when she gets there she goes up

stairs and proceeded to get naked and

hop on Davon.

After they had sex she left. The

next day he called but no answer. He

calls her again but straight to voicemail

He goes to Joe Kush to grab some weed.

When he gets there he comes in and sits

down. "Bro let me grab zip from you" says

Davon. "Baby bring me a zip" says Joe

Kush. Out the room walks Asset, and

Davon heart drops and he stands up.

Asset looks shocked and takes the weed to Joe.

"Here you go bro" says Joe as he hands

Davon the weed. Davon looks at Asset

with a hurt face. Later that night Davon

goes and gets a gun. He goes to Joe

house goes knock on the door and shoots

Joe in the head. He looked for Asset

but she wasn't there. The next day Davon

gets a call.

"Hello" says Davon. "Family what's

good this is Jon I listened to you album

and its fire my guy". "Man that's what's up

how did you get my number". Says Davon.

" I'm connected and I want you to be too.

I wanna sign you to a 1.5 million

dolla deal" says Jon. "Bro are you

serious"? Says Davon. "Yes! That song

"invisible" caught me and my team ear.

Paper work will be to you tomorrow" says

Jon. Just then Davon Mom came to him

and said " the police are ask for you at the

door what happen baby"?

As Davon drops the phone and

heads to the front his heart drops, as he

thinks how much he messed up. They

cuffed him "you are under arrest for the murder of Joseph wilson" says the police. Moral of the story is never let your emotions control your logic. Have faith and don't trust anyone. Focus on yourself before getting into any relationship, and don't play with people emotions.

Chapter 2: The Mother who Cried wolf

Lilith was a woman who was born into a damaged home. Her mom and dad separated because of her mom being unfaithful to her father. Lilth's mom didn't want her father to leave so she threatened him and made life hard for him unless he would be with her. Her father ignored The threats and decided to Leave her alone completely. Due to the fact that her father was now gone she no longer had to ability to have the proper structure in the household. Her mom began to do drugs and also began to take her problems out on Lilith. Lilith was damaged and didn't understand why her Mamma would do the thing that she did. Before the time Lilith went to high school Her mom passed away from doing crack cocaine. She was forced to move in with her aunt. Her aunt did not treat her well she treated her own daughters so much better than she treated Lilth. She struggled for money and, Her aunt would not help. She did not get to experience the love of a mother what a love of a father during her childhood. One day She got pregnant. She was put out Of her aunt's house. She struggled and got assistance as much as she could. Eventually she was able to get a good job. She managed to get a home and take care of her child. As her child began to get older she decided that she was going to get married. The father of the child she had was not in the picture he had passed away years ago. By this time her son had become a high school student.

Being traumatized from her childhood she put a lot of stress on her son as he grew older. She began to beat on him and she began to be frustrated with him when and ignore what he was going through. She did not know how to

express her own thoughts, or frustrations
that she had, so she took it out on him as
her mom did to her when she was a child.
He began to leave home and he began to
get into things that his mom try to get him
not to do from the beginning. He was
forced to grow up and learn a lot of things
that his mom never thought that he would
have to know.

He began to grow wise. Lilth
did not like the fact that when he
will return home from leaving and
come back with the idea that he knew
more than she did. Even though he
actually did understand more than she did
she would not listen to him. One day she
Found little empty bags used to bag
up weed in his pocket, But they was
actually from him selling the weed to

make extra money so that he can be able to do beings some make sure he didn't have to ask her for money. When she confronted him about it he told her that he was selling it and that he did not smoke it which she did not believe him. He stops selling and he tried to do better. He will go to his friends in read The Bible to them and tell them that God had a calling for all of them. His wisdom came from the fact that he will go to church sometimes on Sunday and he was see the Pastor speaking.

The pastor Will speak on things that he seen himself because of his early experience in the street. He would take the information and take it back to his friends. When he went home and he would talk to his mom about it and because his mom told him that she enjoyed to hear about God he will always expect her to be excited. Instead she will be angry that he will be trying to teach her things that she felt like she already knew. As he got older he was trying to make it out. When he graduated from high school he did not have a car. His mom had told him that she would give him a car, But once he graduated she told him that she will only said that because, she wanted him to graduate. He was heartbroken in really didn't understand why she would lie to him about something that he already planned on doing.

As he end up realizing

he needed to leave he left and got his self together and he end up managing to pull a lot together.

At this time Lilith got herself together and she had got into a nice financial situation. When her son would ask for help she would tell him that he had to learn how to get it how she did. She never experienced the love and the ability to get help from her parents. One day he was trying to find a way to come over some real money. He was with some guys and they was trying to steal some TV's out of the house. As they ran out the house the owner of the house came out with a shotgun and shot at them and shot her son in the back n he instantly died. Lilth Got a kick at the door. "Mrs Jones, your son has been killed" say the officer. She had a heartache and died shortly after. Moral of this story, dont let the way people treat you stop you from treating people how you want to be treated. Love your children. One day your kids will teach you so listen to them!

Chapter 3: IM SO CONFUSED

Esau was a man who was born in 2004. He had two wonderful parents who were happily married. They both worked, so often when Esau was around 3 years old he would be left alone with his nanny Beth. Beth would invite her grand child over; his name was Ron. Ron and Esau would always play. "Esau"! Yells Ron".

"What is is Ron" says Esau. " I love you"
Ron says softly". Ron's dad was very
close to his sister and would watch his
sister and her boyfriend. That day Ron
tried to do what he seen his sister do with
her boyfriend with Esau. "I love you too
man, your my best friend " says Esau
confidently. Ron kisses Esau. Esau didn't
resists and Ron hugged Esau. "Thank
Esau" says Ron. "What was that for" says
Esau". "That's how my sister tells her
boyfriend she loves him" says Ron. "Oh
ok" Esau says unsettled. When Esau got
older he would learn that Homosexuality
was something that people looked at as
ok. As he got older he met a guy and they
became close. He thought he loved the
man. They would do everything together.

He felt ok with it because in 2020 everybody is ok with this. As he got older he forgot about the situation when he was a kid. He says the world being open with the LGBT community as his favorite group he stood for something. One day he met a woman who was part of the community and they grew close. He wanted to leave the community. He even left the guy he had met. He wanted to marry the woman. Her name was Faith. Faith took his life and turned it upside down. They started to go to church and they even got married. "Baby you are the very best" says Faith. " no you are! Without you I dont know what I would do bae" Says Esau. " Remember you was gay" Faith says as she busts out in laughter ". "Man it's crazy cuz honestly I dont even see how I could ever have been with a man, and now that I'm close to God I understand why it's wrong" says Esau. Esau thought back and remembered the situation when he was a kid and he felt convicted. That day forward he decided to preach about homosexuality and the reason man grow up thinking it's ok to be gay. He changed so many lives. One day he met a guy who said he looked up to him. His name was Ronald. "Sir I really love your message and I just really want to be a part of your movement" says Ronald. They became friends and one day Esau invited him to the house and at dinner with Esau, Ronald and Faith; Esau poured out his testimony about how he was confused as a child and he end up letting the misunderstanding of a kiss from another

boy influence his judgment and cause him

to believe he was gay. He told him that his

ignorance caused him to think being with

men was ok. "Bullshit" Ronald says in

anger. "Excuse me"! Says Esau. "Cut the

bullshit I came her because I wont let you

lie to yourself or the world" says Ronald. "

You enjoyed that kiss when we were kids

and you are gay. You are lying to your self

boy" Ronald continues with a loud voice.

"What the fuck are you talking about"?

Says Esau. Ronald pulls out a gun and

goes over to faith and makes her

bend over at gun point. Esau yells from

him to stop, but Ronald pulls her pants

down and faith crystal out "Stop please"! "

Don't worry you husband is gay he kissed

me when we were younger and turned my

life around he loved me. He wont mind if

we share" says Ronald with a sinister

smirk. "RON"! IS THAT YOU"? Says Esau.

As Ronald puts his penis in faith she

gasps and Esau charges at him in

anger and Ron shoots him in the head!

Moral of this story is to educate your kids

early. Sexuality is in the minds of our kids.

We must teach our kids what's right and

how Gods wants us to live before satan

gets to them.

Chapter4: The King Who Had To Sacrifice

There once was a king named

Delevonti. He was betrayed by his own

people and forced into slavery. He had a son named Nathan who had a son named Yasha. Nathan let his lust for women and love for alcohol cloud him from thinking about the kingdom at all. The family fell so far away from the kingdom Yasha had a chance to Get the kingdom back the kingdom his ancestors once held. Yasha still had the knowledge of the king and the light of God inside him. Yasha created music, clothing, and books to give the people a piece of him and the people loved it. Yasha struggle because his mother didnt believe he was any different than his father because, Yasha too was emotional and let his emotions drive him to lust and drinking. Yasha didnt stop though.

He continued to do things his father
never did even while lusting over women
and drinking alcohol. He was loved by the
world, but his mom would spread bad
things to people who look highly upon her
son. She slandered him through
ignorance. She didnt realize that was
what she was doing. "He just wont listen
to me. He always drunk and gets loud
when i tell him about hisself" says his
mom to his cousin jacob. Jacob
approached Yasha. "Cuz you alright man"
says Jacob. "Yes sir! Im always good bro
whats the word" says Yasha. "Man you
look rough like you been drinking alot"
Jacob says to bring up the topic. "Wow!
You really on that. Cuz im good im Doing
everything i can to push my brand so i can

build this kingdom back up" Yasha says

with aggression.

"Man alcoholics don't get you no where fam

im just saying and people worried about you"

says jacob. "Bro what people? The only

people who got something to say about

how im living my life are the people

around me who are not believing in me

while im building this kingdom" says

Yasha. "Ok cuz i understand man i do

believe in you though". " No you dont cuz.

You dont support my music and you think

im a hypocrite because i teach people

about God, but i drink. I am only as perfect

as the world i live in, and you out here

scamming people, but act like me

drinking makes me a failure even though

im making money the legal way and in

Gods will, get out my face with that

ignorance" Yasha says. A month later

jacob was arrested while being accused of

identity theft. Yasha's mom called him

and told him about it, but she thought

swore he was innocent even though

Yasha knew the truth. "Baby you need to

get yourself together. If Jacob got locked

up and he's such a good kid aint not

telling Whats going to happen with you

out here living like this" says Yasha's

mom. "Ma im leaving i cant be around you

with this lack of faith in my life. Im not

perfect but i definitely am for the right

things. I drink, because it helps me ignore the fact that im

surrounded by a lack of love and faith."

Yasha left home and he began to meet

people who believed in him and helped

him climb. He became the biggest CEO in

the world. He got the kingdom back. After his success he went home to find out his mom had passed and she never got to see his success. He stopped drinking after that day and started a foundation helping kids build relationships with their family who might not understand the love that is really there. Yasha saved the world from being destroyed by a lack of love.

Moral of the story is no matter what a person indulges in, it will not take away the nature and intent of the person.

Chapter 5: The Golden illness

Jacob was born healthy at birth. After a Vaccine created by the government to target the "christ gene" his brain did not allow him to access some of the abilities his brain was capable of. As Jacob got older he grew very wise and eventually was able to access more of his brain capacity than what the vaccine intended. One thing was wrong. Jacob had very high emotions and his brain wouldn't let him control them as easily as the average person. His mother treated him as he was sick because she always remembered the doctors telling her he was Autistic. The only problem was that Jacob wasn't sick he was made exactly how God intended. The lack of control of his emotions were actually beneficial so that he was able to speak truth and not be ashamed. His mom hated that he would express how he felt about the way she treated

him. Jacob made very good with music, but

She had little faith in her son, and when

people would ask her of his music, she

would not approve. Jacob spoke of God

and all the things he was shown through

the holy spirit, but his mom felt like he had

no right to speak on things when he him

self wasn't perfect. They would argue " ma I'm

just giving you truth that God has shown

me" says Jacob. " You need to ask God to

give your own guidance before you

preach to me, or anyone else" his mom

said in anger. "All im saying is that you

don't support me and thats what's causing

our relationship to fail" Jacob admits. "No

you don't want to do what you should

instead you want to make music and

preach to people, you wont ever get

money without a real Job! Money first"

says his mom. "I am working for God and

its people I meet everyday who supports

me, but they don't even know me, and your

my mother and neglect me" Jacob say

as he leaves.

Jacob was out preaching the word of

God, and a crowd swarmed around him.

"Repent for the Kingdom of God is here!

God has sent us light to use to see our

way out of the darkness" he preached. "I

say with all respect that a poor man on

the street with no knowledge of God will

make it into the kingdom, easier than a

rich man trying! Therefore treat each

person as you would want to be treated

yourself and you too can be part of the

kingdom" he continued to preach and the

crowd grew. The next day he was contacted by a man named Solomon. " sir i have a church that has been looking for a pastor and i would love for you to join us" said Solomon. Jacob immediately accepted the job and began preaching at the church. When Jacob's mom found out she was furious. She started to stand outside after services and telling people not to go. "Do not attend this hypocritical church any more. That man is not mental right, he is my son and he is damaged spreading false doctrines " she yelled out. Jacob found out and had his mom removed from the property. Jacob's church grew into the biggest church in America. His mom got sick. Jacob didn't know of his moms sickness. She didnt want anything to do with him and she was going to die unless she came up with the

money. She was dying from

depression. She was lonely and angery

with her son.

She had to sell her home just to pay

half of the expenses that was needed.

One day she was at the hospital and a

nurse came in and spoke to her. "Why do

you seem so sad, it will not help your

condition " she said. "My life is over with i

have nothing to live for. My own son

became the devil, and left me for dead"

Jacob's mom said in anger. "You know

what i heard not to long ago. It was a boy

who had a mother who hated him and she

would try to tell everybody to avoid her

son. One day the boy became very rich

and he put money in a account for his

mom everyday until the mother would realize how much he loved her and what his true intentions were" the nurse continued. " The mother never reach out to him and he was very sad, and one day the man got married had a child and left his kingdom that he had built to his son. So after he passed" said the nurse.

"What happened to the mother" Jacob's mother asked. " I don't know, his Son told the church that she was very sick and he felt like she would never forgive his father" the said the nurse. "That's the end of the story? Thats not a very good story" Jacobs mom said. "Wait there is my pastor right here" she says as she see's a man in the hall and tells him come in. "This is my pastor he can finish the story for you i dont tell it right, but it reminds of you" says the nurse. "This woman tells me your father died" says Jacob's mom. "Yes. He past a years ago" the man says. "What happened to his mom and why was she so mad" says Jacob's mom. "I never knew why she was mad. My dad always said, she thought he was not smart, and a hypocrite" he said. "Sounds like my son" Jacob's mom says. "You are his mom grandma" says Jacob's son. Jacob's mom was in shock and his son went to hug her and he finally told her everything and the money his dad put up they used for her surgery, and she was healed! She cried so hard after realizing she waited until her son was dead to understand how valuable he was.

Moral of the story, listen to your kids and

have faith that they can be as great as christ

himself, no matter how many mistakes

they make!

Chapter 6: Experience Killer

Charles was a man who had so much

stress. As a child he was abused by his

mother's boyfriend and always

oppressed by him and his mother. He

had no friends, because he couldnt do

anything after school except read books.

His favorite book was the bible. He

began to read the bible so much that he

started to see himself in the stories.

As he got into high school he fell away

from his faith and the church, and began

to disobey his nother by leaving even

when she told him not to. He

experienced much hardship and trials.

He sold drugs to have money and he smoked weed with the people he called his homies. Even though his mom pushed him away to please her mom boyfriend; one thing thing he did want to do is stay in school and finish. His life once he left home was much tougher, and made it hard for him to go to school and still have money, so he would miss school to make money. He eventually got tired of not being able to focus on school and wanted to go back home. When he would return his mother and her boyfriend would make things very hard for him. He felt like a outsider due to the fact his siblings were well treated since birth and he was always the one who had the tough love. One day on his way to bos long distance school in the car with his mother, she said "Hand me my purse". As he hands her the purse she grabs some gum out her bag and throws in back "here" she said. As he put the back down on the floor she was immediately angry that he didnt continue to just hold it so it would be on the floor and she punched him in the jaw very hard, and he immediately got out the car and left to go enroll in his neighborhood school. After that day he moved with his aunt and he to pay her rent. His father had died when he was 13, so he started to receive SSI that his mom kept from him until he turned 16 to get on his own. He used that money to pay rent and buy drugs to sell for extra money to get by each month. By his 12th grade year he was a whole year behind. Through all his struggles he continued to gain knowledge and wisdom, but he was upset, because he would no longer be graduating on time. He picked back up his and started reading again. He immediately remembered his past reading and it came back to him how Wrong he has been. He realized that no matter the choices his mom made, or the hate she showed him that he still was in control of his choices. He realized that if he just dealt with her evil ways just until high school was over things would be better. He end of enrolling in a school that helped him graduate faster than he would have and he went off to a community college and started his next life. When he turned 25 his brother who chose to never leave home and deal with all those things was murdered. He was in tears thinking like how? Why him he did what he should have. His brother wanted until he was 21 to sell drugs and while out selling drugs he was murdered. Charles used that as motivation to change the world and seek a way to help kids who might not have proper guidance. He became a well known leader and changed the world. Moral of the story is, don't regret you choices, because they happen for a reason. Just follow God. Its better to learn and go through things early and make it through, and learn than to wait till later to make mistakes.

Chapter 7: The Holy Ghost

Billy was 6 years old and his teachers told his mom to put him on medication, because he could sit still and class. His mom refused, because she knew other kids who weren't right after taking the prescribed medication. His mom told Billy to start act right in school. Billy was very talkative, and outspoken. His mind always roamed around making it difficult for him to sit still for long periods of time with out having anything to keep he interested. Other kids like Billy were put on medications that stop them from using their full brain compatibility unlike Billy who just got whooping's by his mother when the teacher called on him about his behavior. After years and years of growth and development of understanding himself Billy became very well spoken and got into the word of God. His mental as a child gave him the ability to think about things in ways others had trouble. "Repent for the kingdom of God is here" said Billy. As he preached the word of God the people were amazed and they never saw anyone who could speak the things he did. When Billy was 21 a angel had called him into her presence and anointed him with authority. "You have the Authority"! She said with a powerful voice. After that day Billy was able to do things no other man could. He began to help people. He healed their hearts, and minds allowing them to see clearly the message of God. Many followed him and he lead them to citizenship in the Kingdom of God.

Moral of the story is that there are many kids like Billy right now who have the holy spirit and it doesn't allow for them to be a calm and undergoing as the average kid. Do NOT give them medication to change or alter their mind, it is in Gods well for their ways and behavior. Discipline and teach your children.

Chapter 8: Satans Children

In a small town 2 young men grew up surrounded by thugs, and killers. Elijah and Kane. Elijah was different from everyone else, but him and Kane where best friends. Eventually Elijah family moved and they had to separate. "Bro imma miss you my guy" says kane. "I know dawg imma miss you too bro"

They both had different lives once they separated. Elijah went to school and graduated with honors, and he was into church very hard. He never got too spiritual, because all the things he seen as a kid made him think about alot of things. Kane was in the street and dropped out of school to help his mother with bills. Kane killed people, and even robbed people that was in his way. Kane eventually started making lots of money. One day Elijah was on social media and seen kane and sent him a friend request. Days later kane accepted and sent Elijah his number. Elijah called. "Yo". Said Kane. "Brother whats the deal" Elijah said excitedly. "Man where you at come chop it up wit yo manz". Kane responds. "Bet

imm be out there tomorrow". Replies

Elijah. Elijah was supposed to go off to

college in a month with a full

scholarship to his favorite Historical

Black College, so he was home until

than. He went to visit Kane, and saw that

he had alot of nice things and money.

"Bro you over here winning" says Elijah.

"We bossing up around here thats all

fam" replies Kane. Kane shows Elijah a

very good time and takes him out

around some of his friends and they all

party and have a good time. Elijah who

never have done drugs decided to

smoke and drink with them. He enjoy

him self and the next day he called Kane

to do it all again. Kane says to Elijah "

bro i can put you on, so you can have a

whip of your own like mine, and get you some real money". Elijah hesitate. "Yea put me up bro i need it". Says Elijah. Elijah goes out one night with Kane and he gives Elijah 2 bags of crack. Elijah looked at how tiny they looked and said, "whats this". Kane replied "girl". He told him to go across the street give it to a man standing across from a gas station on the corner of the main street. He ran across gave him the bags and got 40 dollars and ran back across. "Now thats what you do". Says Kane. Elijah after that day got good and start making alot of money. Then one night he went to serve in a neighborhood away from Kanes and handed a man 2 bags but the man only had 30 dollars and was short. Elijah told

him "i cant do that fam i gotta get it all"
the man yelled loud making a bird sound
and ran off, and Elijah got out to pull a
gun on the man and someone came
from behind him and shoot him in the
head and he died. When Kane found out
he went and shot up the whole block,
and as he was leaving the police pulled
up behind him. He didnt stop and kept
going. He drove for 4 blocks and more
police came blocking him off and made
him crash. He was taken to the hospital
and arrested and taken into custody
once he healed.

Moral of this story is that God has his
children and Satan has his children that
he will allow to be ok to keep his work
going. And when one of Gods children
come to Satan side. Satan will take you

out. Stay on your path of God even when you see Satan supplying his children with things you desire. Stay faithful to God's law and all that is promised will come in its time.

Chapter 9: She Get it from her momma

Stephanie was 5 years old when she was exposed to sex. She was taken advantage by her Older cousin. She grew up sexually aroused to things normal girls her age didn't even have knowledge of. Her parents didn't know and she began to do sexual acts with guys as she got in to middle school. She would preform oral sex to guys that had no attention of messing with her. She just wanted to satisfy them and the fact guys would tell other guys she received a lot of attention and sexual experiences. As Stephanie went on to high school she had become popular and would tried to have boyfriends, but guys knew of her back grown and only messed with her to have sex and would leave her alone after. Once she realized that she couldn't find anyone to be with her except for sex she slowed down on being as open with her sex life. Finally she end up graduating and went off to college where she began to date again. In college she didn't know anyone, so she had a fresh start. She decided to become sexually active again but didn't want to only have one man. She was attracted to many men. She had one man who fell in love with her but he couldn't sexually satisfy her, so she decided to keep him, but still seek sex

from other men. One day she got

pregnant by the man that was in love

with her and she end up getting an

abortion, because she didnt want to be

with him. She left him and he was

devastated. She felt bad, but tried to

forget by using guys and sex to distract

her from her emotional guilt. She finally

found a guy she really liked that could

sexually satisfy her, and she feel inlove

with this man. And one day she felt sick

and felt that she might be pregnant

again by this man she fell in love with.

When she went to the doctors they told

her she contracted AIDs and has HIV

and she instantly felt a sharp pain i her

chest. When she told the guy he told her

he didnt think he could pass it with a condom. She was in shock that he didnt tell her he had it and she left the man and spent her last days isolated and depressed.

Moral of this story is to never let sex control your life. Parents teach your kids, ladies respect yourself. Sexual satisfaction isn't the purpose of a relationship, and always treat other how you want to be treated. Learn from your mistakes and seek God.

Chapter 10: Come on now baby momma

Mercedes was a lil girl who grew up in a house with 2 older brothers and a lil sister. She was born prematurely, and this made her mother treat her more delicate than the rest of her children.

Her mother always was over protective of her due to the fact she almost died at birth. Mercedes didnt date much, because she wasnt as developed as the girls her age growing up. She learned about guys from her younger sister, and cousin; who had tremendous problems with males. They were always cheating on their men, and her cousin even took one of Mercedes boy friends. Mercedes began to develop her own perception of life and dating. One day after she graduated and was working for a couple years she was out at a Mall and ran into a guy named James. James was a young man in college who had no Job but a dream to build his own multi billion dollar company. Considering where he came from and what he had the idea seemed far fetched to Mercedes, but she still found interest in him. She would travel a hour a way to see James everyday. One day in the car James said " I cant wait until i finish my first book its going to be crazy, and that's just the start my clothing and music is going to be the next thing poppin". Mercedes responds, saying " You, know that's going to take a lot". "Not more than I'm willing to give" says James. Eventually Mercedes got tired of going to drive and see James, and she bought her a house and insisted that he move in. Mercedes didn't want James to pay anything, because she knew he was jobless. She would buy him weed and make sure they had food and all. James got tired of not having his own, and got a job. One days after James got his second check they got into a argument. "My check is only $215 how do you expect me to give you $150 when you know I'm trying to get in the studio and buy what i need for my clothing line". James cried out. "You cant even look out for me like i look for you that sad, You don't care about me" said Mercedes. It only got worse, because Mercedes mother, and cousin (who stole her last man) would tell her James was using her, because they though he was too good for her that he would want her for her. James got kicked out by Mercedes, but once she felt lonely and thought about the situation she realized she didn't want to lose him, because he did make her happy and he treated her well. James asked her " Are you going to keep kicking me out, because i don't make as much money as you"? "No I'm sorry i was wrong". Said Mercedes. Mercedes let him move back in, but only to do the same exact thing 2 months later once he found a better job. This went on for 2 years, and she got pregnant. By this time James had sold over a hundred T shirts and over hundreds of CD, and books, but also stay with a job. After a serious situation happened at his job that was out of his control Mercedes started talking to another man. When she started to really like the guy she kicked James out again to have the other guy come around. After James realized what had happened he was devastated. The new Guy she met name was West. West had a great Job and amazing newer car, and he had his own kids as well. West and Mercedes started off good, and then west started to beat Mercedes, and she was too embarrassed to say anything, because James told her about the type of men that's out there that wasn't like him. James was a God fearing man. West was not. West would hit her son after he came home drunk and want to watch tv where her son was. She never spoke out about it. She saw James raise to success and get his company finally up and running, and he was able to get him a place and he got a court order for his son to live with him after he noticed bruises on him. Her mom who had to her to leave James, because be was broke

passed away, and broke her soul. After

some years of Mercedes being stuck

she was killed by West, and her family

was devastated. James went on to own

a multi billion company, and his son took

over after he passed to continue the

legacy. Moral of this story, is never lose

faith in a person, because of

circumstances. Never judge a person off

their current situation. And everything

that glitters ain't gold. Water your own

grass, and can becoming green than on

the other side.

Made in the USA
Middletown, DE
22 March 2021